GO FISH

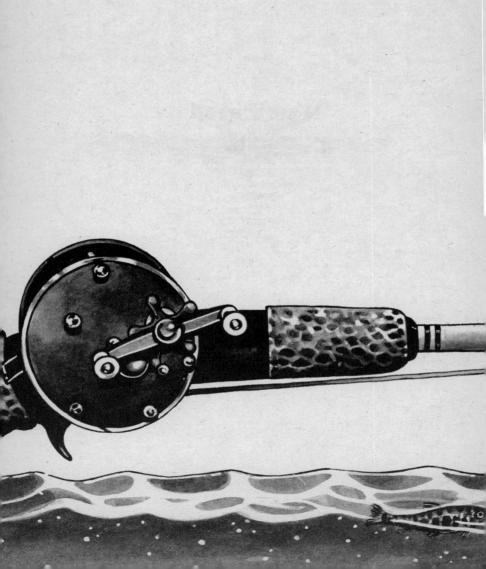

MARY STOLZ
GO FISH

illustrated by
PAT CUMMINGS

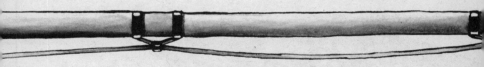

SCHOLASTIC INC.
New York   Toronto   London   Auckland   Sydney
Mexico City   New Delhi   Hong Kong   Buenos Aires

ISBN 439-49707-8

12 11 10 9 8   7/0

Printed in the U.S.A.   40

First Scholastic printing, November 2002

For Three Fisherpeople:
Eliza, Zachary, & Grandfather Bob
—M.S.

To Robert Warren
—P.C.

CHAPTER 1

Grandfather was in his favorite armchair, reading a book.

Thomas was trying not to interrupt.

"Where's Ringo, I wonder," he said, and added, "I'm talking to myself, Grandfather. Not to you."

Grandfather went on reading.

"Gone someplace, probably," said Thomas. "Some secret cat place that we don't know about." He looked around the room, hoping to find something of interest.

1

His bat and ball were against the wall, but he wouldn't be able to play for a while yet. He'd broken his ankle trying to steal second, and Dr. Hoskins had taken off the walking cast only yesterday.

"Did you hear Dr. Hoskins tell me to try for the pitcher's spot?" Thomas asked. "He says everybody wants a lefty hurler. What do you say to that, huh, Grandfather? Do you think that's maybe a good idea?"

Grandfather didn't hear. Or didn't listen.

Thomas liked to read. Not as much as Grandfather did. He supposed no one else in the whole world liked to read that much. Still—he had his own books in his room, and some of them were pretty good. A big book about dinosaurs was his favorite. He liked to think of them stomping over the land, millions and millions of years ago. *That* would have been something to see. The earth would crack under those tons of weight, and their huge tails would dig trenches in the ground. A

2

dinosaur could have lived *right here in Florida where he and Grandfather lived now.* Thomas could picture it standing out in the backyard, turning its little head from side to side, gazing across the Gulf of Mexico while it nibbled away the tops of trees.

"Dinosaurs ate salads—did you know that, Grandfather? They made them out of trees and ferns and different kinds of moss. Like we make ours out of lettuce and tomatoes and broccoli and stuff. That's pretty interesting, I'd say." After a pause—"Wouldn't you say that was interesting?"

No sound from the armchair.

It was much too good a day to sit indoors looking at words and pictures, even about dinosaurs. There might be something on television to watch, only it was too early for that. Grandfather said television before five o'clock in the afternoon would stunt his growth.

Thomas thought about that and laughed. "You sure say funny things, Grandfather," he observed, lifting his voice a little. After a bit he sighed and got up from the floor, where he'd been lying on his back watching a green lizard whisk across the ceiling.

He went to the kitchen for a glass of milk. He didn't exactly want one, but it was something to do.

He pulled the bottle from the refrigerator and dropped it, spilling milk over the linoleum. Unluckily, he had not put the cap on tight the last time he'd taken a drink. Luckily, the bottle was plastic. Besides, there was hardly any milk left in it.

"Oh, baloney!" he called out. "Now see what's happened!"

No response from Grandfather.

"I suppose I ought to mop this up? Unless maybe you'd do a better job of it, Grandfather? Sometimes I don't clean things just the way you want me to. Maybe I shouldn't even start if you think it'd be better for you to do it. I'm just asking."

Grandfather stirred but made no answer.

"Okay," Thomas grumbled. "I'll do it myself."

He opened the door of the cupboard under the sink, yanked out a sponge, banged the cupboard door, slapped the sponge onto the floor, got to his knees, and sloshed and washed up the milk.

"This isn't easy," he explained in a loud voice.

Ringo put his nose to the kitchen screen door. "Let me *in*," he cried. "I've been out here for *hours*!"

Thomas smiled and opened the door. In came his big white cat, whining and twining. Complaining. Grandfather often said he'd never known how talkative a cat could be until they got Ringo. "Or," he'd usually add, "until he got us."

□ □ □

Ringo had appeared, a couple of years back, on a rainy April night, crying at the back door. "I'm a *kitten*!" he'd called in a small, mewing voice. "I'm this *lost* kitten that somebody has to *do* something about!"

Leaping from the floor, where he spent a lot of time, Thomas ran to open the door. "Lookit!" he yelled. "Look, Grandfather, at this kitty that's all wet out in the rain!"

His grandfather, who'd been getting ready for bed, came to the door, frowning. "We don't need a cat."

"I think he needs us."

Grandfather turned his hands up. "You have a way of putting things, Thomas, that I have no way to answer, except to say that you're right. I'll get a towel, and you find something for it to eat. There's some flounder left from dinner."

That was how Ringo had come to live with them. From a small complaining kitten he had grown to be a large complaining cat.

Thomas carried on conversations with him.

"How can you tell what he's talking about?" Grandfather once asked. "It's all meow to me."

"Easy," Thomas explained. "He's either asking to be let out if he's in, or in if he's out, and the rest of the time he's explaining how hungry he is. He thinks we starve him."

Grandfather lifted his eyes. "He should look in the mirror."

□ □ □

Now, with his small pink tongue, Ringo helped Thomas to clean up the milk.

"That's *good*," Thomas said to him. Ringo liked some words to be said low, and some louder. He especially liked a squealy voice.

"A *very* good job, Ringo-Bingo-Singo-*Bam*!" said Thomas in that kind of voice.

Ringo wound around himself with pleasure. He fell to the floor, which by this time was pretty clean, if sticky, and rolled onto his back, eyes half closed, purring like a small outboard motor.

Thomas went into the living room, slapped his hands together, and said, "There! All taken care of, Grandfather. Ringo helped. I would've been a long time, just doing the whole entire job by myself."

Ringo jumped to the back of Grandfather's chair, put his nose against Grandfather's ear, and whispered a few purring words. Grandfather's grip on his book tightened.

Thomas poked around, looking at things. Even when he thought he'd already seen all of Grandfather's interesting stuff, every time he looked, he found something else he'd either overlooked or forgot about.

"Hey, Grandfather," he said. "When did you get this new piece of driftwood? It looks like a snake, doesn't it—kind of slithery? Except how could a piece of wood slither, huh? *That's* a pretty funny idea. I just had it. Well, I couldn't have had it before, of course, because I just now saw this new piece of driftwood you must've found yesterday or sometime like that...."

Grandfather brought his book up till his whole face was hidden.

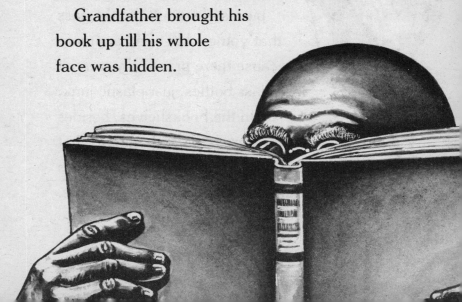

Thomas sauntered about, hands behind his back.

Over the years, Grandfather had collected, or made, all kinds of things. He had a cabinet of shells from the beaches of Florida. They ranged from the tiniest, a wentletrap about the size of a pencil point, to a huge lightning whelk that Thomas and Grandfather had measured and found to be a foot and three inches long. Grandfather collected stones of curious shapes, and bits of petrified wood, and pieces of smooth bottle glass that you couldn't find anymore because there practically weren't any glass bottles, just plastic junk. On the bookshelves, besides books, were birds and animals that Grandfather had carved from beach stones and driftwood that had washed ashore.

10

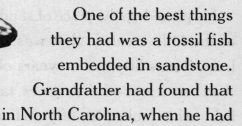

One of the best things
they had was a fossil fish
embedded in sandstone.
Grandfather had found that
in North Carolina, when he had
been a boy himself, just about
the age Thomas was now. Eight.

Everybody old had once been
young. That was a fact.
Everyone in the
world—even the oldest
person, even people older than
Grandfather—had started out as a baby.

Of course Thomas knew this, but it was one of
those things he knew, and could not
make himself
believe.

He picked up the piece of sandstone and stared at the little creature that was not even an inch long. It was fifty million years old. Maybe older. And here it was—head, bones, tail—a perfect tiny fish, being looked at, fifty million years later, by this person, Thomas.

Whenever he looked at it, he got nearly tongue-tied with wonder. This very fish had swum in an ocean that had once covered, Grandfather said, all the eastern seaboard of America. This fish that he held in his hand had swum in that ancient sea and when it died had got captured forever in layers of sandstone, to be found after fifty million years, maybe more, by a boy who was now Thomas's grandfather. It was easier to believe in dinosaurs that he couldn't see than in this fossil he saw every day.

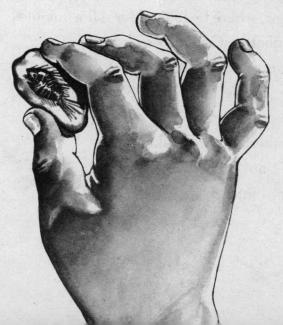

Putting it down, he took up one of Grandfather's birds—a green heron carved out of a piece of teak. He moved it from the mantel to a table. He sat at the table and got out a deck of cards. With a glance at the armchair, he began shuffling.

Grandfather lowered his book and glared across the room.

Smiling, Thomas walked back to the kitchen, looked out the window, and shouted, "Grandfather! Hey, Grandfather! It's SNOWING!"

Into the kitchen tramped his grandfather, over to the window, where he looked for a few minutes toward the glinting Gulf of Mexico.

"Well," he said. "Well, well. No snow at the back of the house, Thomas. Shall we try the front?"

"Grandfather! You're making fun."

"Certainly not. If it's snowing around here, I intend to see it."

14

They walked through the living room, opened
the front door, stepped out onto the porch.
Ringo went with them. He leaped to the
railing, tucked his paws beneath his
chest, and closed his eyes.

In the front yard hibiscus
bushes were in bloom, and bougainvillea
climbed along the fence. A huge live oak spread
its leafy branches, providing shade, sheltering
nests. A crow crouched in the birdbath.
He was too big for it, but flapped his
wings happily. Bits of
rainbow flashed
through his
splashings.

Grandfather said, "What do you know? It stopped snowing before I got to make a snowball."

"Grandfather, you *are* making fun. Anyway, I didn't say where it was snowing, did I?"

"Ah. You mean that somewhere in the wide world, at this moment, as you and I stand here, snow is falling."

"Of course," said Thomas, and added, "Isn't it?"

"Of course."

"I suppose it *could* snow here, someday."

"I suppose you could suppose that. To be on the safe side we'll buy you a sled."

"Oh, *Grandfather*," Thomas said, laughing.

"Tell me . . . do you plan to interrupt my reading for the rest of the morning?"

"Well . . ."

Grandfather nodded. "I thought as much."

He went back to the living room and put a marker in his book.

"Thomas," he said.

"Yes, Grandfather?"

"Let's go fishing."

CHAPTER 2

They got their equipment together.

1. Two rods with reels.

2. A tackle box containing hooks, lead weights the size of BBs, and the pliers they used to snap the weights to the lines. The pliers also had cutters to cut the line if they caught a fish too big to handle. This had not happened to them yet.

3. A landing net.

4. A cast net for catching bait fish.

5. A pail to keep the bait fish in, once Grandfather had caught them in the cast net.

6. A five-gallon bucket to put water in to keep their fish in once they'd caught them.

7. A bottle of sunscreen.

8. A tape to measure a fish they were not sure was big enough to keep.

9. A scale for weighing a fish that looked big enough to weigh and list in their record book.

They did not often catch fish this big, and there were few notations in the book:

Sheepshead over ten pounds, three entries.

Redfish over ten pounds, five entries.

And, most memorable, with a page all to itself, a sixteen-pound snook caught last year, in the proper season, by Grandfather.

"There we are," Grandfather said now. "I guess that's everything."

They put on their beaked caps and started off, clanking. Ringo kept them company to the place where the lane gave way to a path leading down to the beach through sea oats, sea grapes, and sand spurs. Then he'd return to his railing perch and wait for a fish dinner.

At the edge of the Gulf, shallow waves slid over the sand and retreated, leaving winks of foam where coquinas burrowed to safety, then emerged with the next wave's wash. Sometimes Grandfather and Thomas collected a bucket of the tiny bivalves to make a broth for gumbo.

Walking half a mile, they came to an old wooden pier jutting out into the water. There had been a house here, many years before. A hurricane had swept it out to sea, most strangely leaving the dock behind.

Underneath the dock, stretching a long way on both sides, were tremendous rocks that had formed a seawall to protect the house that was no longer there. The seawall had failed to hold back heavy tides in that long-ago hurricane, a storm that had drowned landmarks, toppled water towers, and wrenched trees up by the roots. After tearing highways from their beds, throwing houses out to sea, it had raged away, leaving all that wrack behind.

Grandfather's own house had been almost buried. In their album were snapshots that showed a huge bough lying across the roof, a branch sticking into what was now Thomas's bedroom. A tremendous dune, mixed with shells and seaweed, was piled against the front door. This had happened in the *before-you-were-born-Thomas* times.

Thomas tried to imagine a world that he, his very own self, wasn't part of—a world that people had been going up and down in, doing the things people do, a world where *Grandfather* had been a boy himself, with a grandfather of his own, and where *that* grandfather had had *his* grandfather, and you could keep going back like that until, as Grandfather often said, you were face to face with a long-long-long-ago ancestor in Benin, an ancient town in Africa. And none of those people knowing a thing about Thomas.

Well, it was strange.

Thomas liked to hear stories about those times. But even as he was listening to and believing Grandfather's tales, he couldn't make himself *know* that there had once been a world without him in it. It was as hard to believe as that North Carolina had been at the bottom of the ocean, or that the tiny fossil fish on Grandfather's desk had lived and swum in and died in that ocean, fifty million years ago.

"Isn't the world *strange*, Grandfather?" he would say from time to time, and his grandfather always agreed that it was strange indeed.

At low tide, the rocks that remained of the former seawall stood out of the water, covered with barnacles and sea grass, crawling with ocean life. Crabs. Sea snakes. Large, glossy, seafaring cockroaches that made Thomas shudder.

24

"Why did there have to be cockroaches?" he'd asked his grandfather, who answered that because a creature seems ugly doesn't mean it has no right to exist.

"What do you mean, *seems*?" Thomas had demanded.

"No doubt cockroaches consider one another handsome."

"Humph," Thomas said. There were times when he didn't understand his grandfather.

But now it was almost high tide and the rocks were covered.

Looking down, Thomas spied a school of glass minnows glinting near the sunken wall. They swam in formation, like soldiers, darting forward all together, then—*about-face*—off in a different direction. Grandfather said that in this way they fooled hungry predators, who thought they were one enormous fish instead of thousands of very little ones.

"You wouldn't think fish could be so smart," Thomas said.

"Everything in nature is smart when it comes to staying alive as long as possible," said Grandfather.

"I guess that's right," said Thomas. He thought of the coquinas trying to escape into the sand before some crab or heron got them. Or before he and his grandfather scooped them up to make a broth out of.

Everything alive, trying to stay alive. He looked at the minnows, soon to be bait. They were about the size of Grandfather's fossil fish.

"Do you suppose any of these guys will get to be fossils?" he asked.

"Little chance of that. There are too many fishermen around. Like us."

"Fifty million years ago there weren't an awful lot of fishermen, I guess."

"There weren't *any*," said Grandfather. "Human beings, including fishermen, had not yet appeared on our planet in those long-ago times."

"Golly," said Thomas.

Grandfather was always telling him things that took an effort to understand. This time he decided not to try. "Don't you sometimes feel sorry for all these poor little minnows and shiners? I mean, besides not getting to be fossils, they don't have a chance against *us*. Or the big fish that're after them."

28

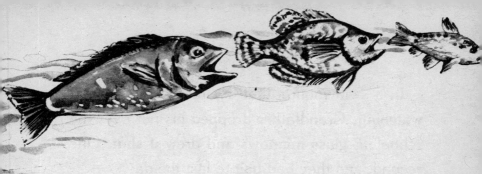

"That's how it is, Thomas. Everything has to eat. Human beings, fish, birds, animals. It means all of us trying to catch something that doesn't want to get eaten."

"Not all of us," said Thomas. "I mean—like cows. They eat just grass. And my friend Donny—his family eats only vegetables. They're vegetarians. Like dinosaurs," he added, in case he hadn't made himself clear.

"Not all dinosaurs were vegetarians," Grandfather said. Thomas didn't hear him. He was lying on his stomach, leaning over the dock to dip the bait bucket full of water while Grandfather got the cast net ready, flicking the weights expertly into place, holding the lead line in his teeth.

In a swift motion that Thomas never tired of watching, Grandfather dropped his net over the schooling glass minnows and drew it shut. One second, and they had bait to last the day.

A great blue heron appeared squawking from the trees behind them. Stooping on wide wings, he landed, feet forward, at the end of the pier, where he stood unmoving as one of Grandfather's carvings, except for his plumes that stirred in a slight breeze. After a while he moved toward them on skinny legs with knobby knees that angled backward. Making progress in slow motion, he arrived at the bucket of minnows. Thomas and Grandfather watched as he dipped his swordlike beak and daintily selected a fish. His neck looped as he tossed it down and reached for another.

"Put the lid on," said Grandfather after the heron's third minnow had been gulped down. "We came here to get our dinner, not to supply him with his."

□ □ □

There was this about fishing, Thomas thought: It was fun—if you didn't think how the fish felt about it—and it provided him and his grandfather with food a good part of the year.

"Are we poor?" he asked, as Grandfather baited both rods.

"Not exactly."

"Are we rich?"

"Not exactly."

"We're in between?"

"More toward the poor end. I'd call us semi-poor."

"Well, that's okay," said Thomas. He waited as Grandfather cast for him, then took his rod and moved it up and down in a gently jerky motion.

"I hope I catch one," he said.

"Me, too," said Grandfather.

□ □ □

Time passed.

The heron stood quietly, his plumes fluttering.

White clouds rose in the sky like chalk castles.

A large transparent jellyfish, palely green, pumped along the surface of the water.

"Remember when you used to call those Jell-O fish?" asked Grandfather.

A little annoyed, Thomas said, "That was *ages* ago."

"Of course," said Grandfather. He added, "It was a good description. Doesn't that fellow look like a bowl of lime Jello-O floating along?"

"He isn't green enough," said Thomas.

"Picky," said Grandfather.

A stingray went by beneath them, rippling like ribbons. Out in the Gulf a school of porpoises arched toward the sky and curved again into the sea, over and over.

Three pelicans arrived, splashing close to the pier, where they bobbed up and down, looking up at Thomas and Grandfather in hopeful silence.

"They remind me of little Viking ships, the way they're shaped," said Grandfather. He always said that.

Thomas took three shiners from the bucket and tried to toss one to each of the pleading pelicans, but the yellow-headed one got all three.

"Oh, gee," said Thomas. "I better try again."

"I think not," said Grandfather. "They're better fishermen than we are, and you may be sure they'd not share their catch with us."

After what seemed to Thomas a very long time, he said, "I don't think we're going to catch anything, Grandfather."

"The most important thing in fishing," said Grandfather, "is patience."

He always said that, too.

Thomas sighed. He yawned. He flicked his line gently and tried to be patient.

CHAPTER 3

"How *long* do we have to be patient?" Thomas asked.

"As long as it takes," said Grandfather.

This didn't sound good. Thomas scowled, scratched his arm, his head, his ankle. He shifted from one leg to the other.

"Observe, Thomas, how quietly they wait—the pelicans and our friend the heron. They don't wriggle and writhe, like some I could name."

"They don't have anything to do but wait."

"Thomas, I've said it before and I say it again, you are a restless boy."

"I know," Thomas said. "Grandfather?"

"Yes, Thomas?"

"When you were a boy, were you restless?"

Grandfather tipped his head till his beard pointed at the sky. "I'll cast my mind back."

Thomas waited.

Grandfather lowered his chin, looked into Thomas's eyes. "I was," he said.

"Oh, good."

Grandfather threw out their lines again, handed Thomas his pole. They went on being patient.

They'd had a few strikes, but each time the fish got the bait and Thomas and Grandfather got nothing.

"All part of the game," Grandfather would say, calmly rebaiting.

Thomas landed a blowfish. It came out of the water already starting on its defense. Breathing deeply, it began to puff up, swelling until it looked like a bubblegum bubble with spines.

"Thinks he looks pretty fierce, doesn't he, Grandfather?"

"He *does* look fierce, for a fellow his size." Grandfather dropped the stiff little blown-up blowfish into the water, where it slimmed down and swam off as if nothing unusual had happened.

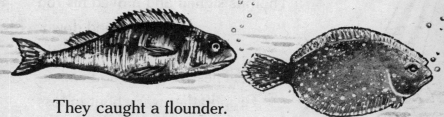

They caught a flounder.

Flounder are bottom fish, and mostly spend their lives buried in sand. Their eyes are on top of their heads, they are flat as plates, and the one they caught was too small to keep. Carefully, Grandfather slid it back into the water. Too bad. Flounder were good eating. Especially the way Grandfather prepared them.

Thinking about Grandfather's cooking made Thomas's mouth water.

"You're a very good cook, Grandfather," he
said.

"True."

"I'm getting kind of hungry."

"So am I," said Grandfather. He did not sound
ready to quit.

Thomas sighed and moved his rod
gently up and down.
They caught a ladyfish.
These are not good eating.
Grandfather was about to toss
it back when the heron
darted forward and took it
right from his hand, then
tossed his head up and
set about swallowing.
Thomas watched as the bony fish
went down the bird's long neck.
"I'm glad we don't have to swallow
whole fish that way," he said.
"So am I," said Grandfather.

40

Suddenly Thomas's rod dipped. A fish flipped out of the water a long way off.

"Speckled trout," said Grandfather. "A big one. Gently, now, Thomas. You don't want him to throw the hook."

"I'm trying," Thomas said, turning the reel as slowly as he could. He wished Grandfather would take over, but didn't ask.

Grandfather believed it was every man to his own fish.

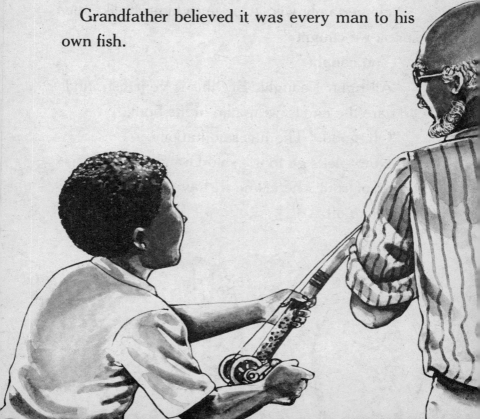

Slowly, slowly, he reeled in his trout until it was close enough for Grandfather to scoop up with the net. He was willing to do that.

"By golly, Thomas!" he shouted. "Look at the size of him!"

Thomas, swelling like a blowfish, regarded his catch proudly. "He'll have to go in the book, won't he, Grandfather?"

"He certainly will. A page to himself, like the snook we caught."

"You caught."

"All right. I caught. But this is your fish, and you are the one to write him in the book."

"Oh, good," Thomas said happily.

"Now—let's go to it," said Grandfather. "This crowd of trout is here, and we have to strike before they take off...."

In the excitement, Thomas forgot to be tired.

Side by side, he and his grandfather caught fifteen trout and had to send only three of them back to sea—to grow bigger and maybe be caught another day.

Twelve good-sized fish. Grandfather would keep out enough for tonight and tomorrow's dinner, and freeze the rest for later eating.

Thomas swallowed hungrily, thinking about dinner.

"All right," Grandfather said at last. "Let's go home."

Collecting their gear, richer by twelve speckled trout, they clanked back up the beach.

CHAPTER 4

Ringo, a cat who knew when fishing had been going on, stalked along the porch railing and jumped to the floor. Twining around Grandfather's legs, he asked for his share.

"I'm *starving*," he cried in a mewful voice. "I'm dying of *hunger*, nobody ever *feeds* me...."

Grandfather, not impressed, put the fish in a plastic bag, and put the bag in the refrigerator. He'd wait till they were cold to fillet them.

"Thomas," he said, "please explain to your cat that he's obliged to wait till dinnertime, like the rest of us."

Thomas looked at the kitchen clock. Years back, Grandfather had taught him to tell time on clocks with hands. A lot of his friends, like Donny, could read only digital clocks.

Hands straight up. Twelve noon.

"It's ages till dinner, Grandfather."

Grandfather was unmoved. "Lunch will hold you."

They had peanut-butter sandwiches and milk and apples. Ringo, who was supposed to eat only twice a day, had a small dish of cat kibble.

"It doesn't look right," Grandfather sometimes said, "for us to have lunch and tell him that cats can't."

Lunch over, Grandfather retired to his room for a snooze.

Thomas rode his skateboard down the road to Donny's house.

Donny's mother greeted him at the door. "Come in, come in, Thomas," she said. "Where have you been all morning?"

She wouldn't care to hear about fishing. Nobody in Donny's family wanted to know that any creature, any fish or bird or beast, was taken by human beings for the table.

"Just fooling around," Thomas said. At times it seemed you had to say a thing that wasn't true in order not to upset people.

Was that fibbing? he'd asked. Or was it being polite?

"It's both," Grandfather said. "The ideal is to tell nothing but the truth. But perfect honesty at times comes out to perfect rudeness. Or thoughtlessness. Our problem is to know when which is which." He thought that over and added, "If you see what I mean."

"I think I do," Thomas had said, giving his grandfather's arm a comforting pat.

He and Donny spent the afternoon on their skateboards, and when he got home Grandfather was in the kitchen, with the trout already filleted.

Now Ringo got his share, two fish heads that he was invited to enjoy in the backyard.

Dipping the fillets in milk, Grandfather rolled them in seasoned cornmeal, then put them aside while he steamed the broccoli and cooked the rice.

Thomas set the table.

When everything else was ready, Grandfather fried their trout to a crackly brown. Thomas closed his eyes, sniffing the fragrance. He supposed nothing else in the world smelled as good as this. Except when Grandfather baked bread, which he did every Monday.

"Dinner!" Grandfather announced, putting a wedge of lemon on warm plates, then the fish, the broccoli, and the rice. Thomas put a basket of bread on the table. "Oh boy," he said. "I can hardly wait."

"You don't have to," said Grandfather.

For dessert they had mango ice cream and gingersnaps. All homemade by Grandfather. When the last bite was gone, Grandfather patted his stomach. "A dinner fit for a couple of kings, wouldn't you say?"

"What are we going to do now?"

"The dishes."

"I mean after. Are you going to read your book some more?"

"What would you like to do?"

Thomas sat at the table, opened a drawer, and got out their deck of cards.

"Good," said his grandfather. "I like to have my mind made up for me, now and then."

As Thomas picked up the cards, their attention was caught by Ringo, who began to run back and forth along the baseboard, chanting and lashing his tail. With a sudden cry, he leaped up the wall, fell back, and crouched, quivering, eyes fixed on the ceiling.

Grandfather and Thomas looked up.

"The skink again," said Thomas.

For a couple of days, a skink, a lizard about a sixteenth of an inch in circumference and perhaps

50

an inch long, had been occupying a corner of
the room above the bookcases. She would
disappear into the molding, peep out,
pop back, emerge and race across the
ceiling, then rush back to sanctuary.
Ringo, apparently thinking he was
on safari, would scarcely leave
the house, so intent he was
upon the chase.

"Clearly," Grandfather said, "that tiny creature, in her atom of a brain, has reasoned that the whisker-twitching, tail-swinging, crazy-eyed, chattering creature down here on the floor represents danger. So she's sensibly decided to remain up there on the ceiling."

"It's almost as if she's teasing him."

"Does seem that way, doesn't it? I doubt if she's up to anything so complicated as a game of cat and skink."

"You're always telling me how patient animals are, Grandfather, but I don't think Ringo is being patient. He's acting cuckoo."

"That's because he *sees* the prey, right there within what he won't admit isn't springing distance."

"Silly cat," Thomas said fondly.

"Oh, no. It's just that his instinct is stronger than his judgment. But you'll see, Thomas. When the lizard disappears again, he'll settle down to watch for her, quiet as you please."

Just then the lizard slipped behind the molding. For a moment Ringo studied the corner where she dwelt, then leaped to the top of Grandfather's chair and subsided, to wait.

"See?" said Grandfather. And then, "Are you going to deal?"

Thomas dealt. He frowned at his cards. "Do you have any threes?" he asked.

Grandfather tipped up his beard. He lowered his chin. He leaned forward. He tapped his forehead and scowled and muttered.

"Grandfather," Thomas said sternly. "You know if you have threes."

"Give me time. I'm still looking."

Thomas smiled.

After a pretty long time, Grandfather said, "Go fish!"

Thomas, who'd been waiting for this, gave a yell that sent Ringo flying across the room.

"We already did!" he whooped. "Grandfather, we already did GO FISH!"

He thought they'd never stop laughing.

"Grandfather," he said.

"Yes, Thomas?"

"Did you ever see snow? I mean, personally, your own self?"

"Yup."

"Do you think I will, one day? I mean, will I get to see all the places and things that you saw?"

"Thomas, you will see snow, and all the places and things that I saw. You will see more—much more."

"You think so?"

"I know so."

Thomas could hardly imagine it, but if Grandfather said so, then so it would be.

"Did you have a sled?" he asked.

"I didn't own one, but I spent days on my cousin's, up in New York State, where he lived. It was called a Flexible Flyer."

"Oh, my," said Thomas with a sigh. "When was that, Grandfather?"

"Ages ago. In another lifetime."

"Did you have another lifetime?"

"Everybody has."

"What does that mean?"

"Maybe I can explain. I'll try. You see, Thomas, there is the lifetime of childhood, of being a boy. Or a girl, as the case may be. That lasts a long time. When you're in it, you are quite sure it will never end. Then comes the time of being a young person, and after that a middle-aged person. Those are the years when you go along just *being*, if you see what I mean."

"Sort of," said Thomas. "How long does that last?"

"Not quite so long as childhood."

"Then what?"

"The last of all. The lifetime of being old. Like me."

"You aren't so old."

Grandfather picked up his cards. "Do you have any jacks?"

CHAPTER 5

After the card game, they consulted the TV section of the newspaper. Finding nothing that Grandfather said they wanted to see, they went out to the porch and sat on the swing, creaking idly back and forth. Ringo, abandoning the lizard, followed and resumed his railing perch.

The sun flew citrus-colored banners as it sank into the Gulf of Mexico. Cradle songs fell from leafy branches, and crickets scraped their fiddles in the grass. On the ground a pair of mockingbirds hopped around each other, flicking their tails, then lost interest and flew apart. Ringo watched, but made no move toward them.

□ □ □

Thomas yawned. "You could tell me a story," he said.

"All right. What about?"

"You pick. Only not a bad one."

"Do I ever tell you a bad story?"

"I guess I mean not a sad one."

"I see. Only happy people with happy problems, as the old saying goes?"

"Grandfather! That sounds silly."

"It is silly. I try to tell you about life, and life is not full of happy people with happy problems."

Thomas turned and looked into his grandfather's eyes. "I know that already," he said. "I've known that for a long time."

Grandfather put his arm around Thomas and held him close. "Of course," he said, with a whistly sigh. "We know that, don't we?"

Thomas leaned his head against the thin chest.

"Did your grandfather tell you stories?" he asked.

"He did."

"And did his grandfather tell him stories?"

"Yes."

"And did—"

"You could keep that up till we were face to face with your great-great-great-and-one-more-great-grandfather. He who was taken a slave from his home in Benin."

"In Africa."

"Yes. Would you like to hear an African story?"

"Yes. But make it up, please."

According to Grandfather, *his* great-grand-
father had said all the family on that side was
descended from the Yorubas, from that great-
great-great-and-one-more-great-grandfather and
his long-ago wife. Grandfather had a store of
African tales, mostly Yoruban, passed down the
generations since then. He told true stories, which
were history. And folktales, which were mythol-
ogy. *And* he had a gift for making up stories.
Thomas usually liked those best.

It seemed to him that perfect truth, like perfect
honesty, came out sometimes to perfect misery.

"Make one up," he said again, and yawned.

Grandfather tipped his head back, thought for a
few minutes, and began:

"You must understand, Thomas, that certain

Yoruba tribes had the cult of *ibeji*."

Thomas sighed happily. African words!

Iguneromwo. Ikegobo. Uhumwelao. He didn't always remember what they meant, but loved the sound of them.

"What's a cult?" he asked.

"A belief."

"I see. What is *ibeji*?"

"*Ibeji* are twins."

"I see. Go on with the story."

"If I'm permitted to. The cult of *ibeji* held that twins were unlucky for the tribe. Therefore such children were always separated, one sent to a village east, the other to a village west of the village where they were born."

"Why?"

63

"Thomas, I don't *know* why. It's just what my grandfather said his grandfather said his grandfather—and so on back—said was fact. Shall I continue?"

"Oh, yes."

"Fine. Now, let's see." Again Grandfather paused to gather his thoughts. He made up his stories as he went along, which required a certain amount of thinking. Thomas tried to wait patiently.

"All right, here it is, Thomas. Once upon a time, long long ago, in the beginning of the world, Shango, the thunder god, and his wife—"

"What was her name?"

Grandfather exhaled a breath. "Her name was—was Esigie."

"You're making that up."

"I'm making the whole thing up."

"Go on," said Thomas, trying to stifle another yawn.

"Very well. Esigie gave birth to a pair of sons. Twins. Knowing that misfortune would befall the tribe if the twins, the *ibeji*, remained together, Shango transformed them into two winds, sending one to the east and the other to the west of the place where he and Esigie made their home."

Thomas's eyes drooped.
His grandfather's voice seemed
far away. "What happened then?"
he murmured.

"The brothers, the east wind and the west wind,
wanted to come together again, and that is why
they blow around the world to this day, always
trying to find each other but never able to."

"Poor *ibeji*," said Thomas, dropping into sleep.

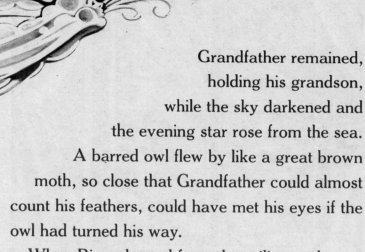

Grandfather remained,
holding his grandson,
while the sky darkened and
the evening star rose from the sea.
A barred owl flew by like a great brown
moth, so close that Grandfather could almost
count his feathers, could have met his eyes if the
owl had turned his way.

When Ringo leaped from the railing and
disappeared into the cricket-humming
garden, and the kitchen clock,
only a minute or so behind the
bell of the Congregational church,
tolled nine o'clock, he gently
awakened Thomas and
steered him
toward
bed.

CHAPTER 6

By the time he'd got into his pajamas and washed up, Thomas was wide awake again. Lying in bed, Ringo on the pillow beside him, he listened to the clattering fronds of a palm tree outside his window. The wind was from the southeast, a rain wind, but there was no rain.

He lay with his hands beneath his head and thought about the brother winds, the east wind and the west wind—the *ibeji*—blowing around the world forever, trying to find each other.

That was a good story. All of Grandfather's

stories were good, the true ones and the made-up ones.

He thought about today. Summer days were long, long days, yet they seemed to go so fast. Grandfather said that when a person was a child, he thought that was what he would always be. It did seem to Thomas pretty crazy to think of himself being anyone but himself, a person his age.

Still, he was beginning, not *quite* believing it but almost, to admit that he would get older.

One day, he would be a grown-up.

He would even be, one day, like his grandfather, *old*.

He wondered if then he would sit with some boy or girl who was his own grandchild, telling tales of long ago, stories of life with Grandfather....

He would tell how they had talked together and fished together, and cooked good meals, and in the evening played cards. He would show his grandchild the album with the picture of Grandfather's house almost buried by the hurricane. There were pictures of Ringo in the album, and pictures of himself and Donny.

How much he was going to have to show and explain!

He would give his grandchild the fossil fish, and tell how *his* grandfather had found it long long ago in North Carolina, though he would point out that "long long ago," in human terms, was nothing compared to the history of a fifty-million-year old fossil.

He would tell, over again, to this grandchild the stories Grandfather had told him. That *his* grandfather had told him, that *his* grandfather had told him... and so back and back, back through the years to Benin, an ancient town in Africa.

He would remember all Grandfather's tales, the true ones and the made-up ones.

Turning over, he pushed his face into the pillow. Ringo climbed on his back and settled there purring. In a sudden rush, rain came crashing through the palm fronds, sounding like wire whisks sliding over a drumhead. And to that music Thomas tried to picture himself, an old man on a porch swing, turning his beard up while he took time to invent a tale to tell the child who sat beside him, waiting for the story to begin....